Joseph Pullen Collins

War

And other Poems

Joseph Pullen Collins

War
And other Poems

ISBN/EAN: 9783337232160

Printed in Europe, USA, Canada, Australia, Japan

Cover: Foto ©Andreas Hilbeck / pixelio.de

More available books at **www.hansebooks.com**

W A R,

AND

OTHER POEMS.

BY

JOSEPH PULLEN COLLINS,

of The Marriage Ode, Mr. Smith's Intended, Who Stops the Way,
The May Queen, To be left till called for, To be disposed of,
The Fly Papers, &c.

LONDON:

ROBT. COULCHER, 50, CHANCERY LANE.

1871.

PREFACE.

In presenting to the public some of my earliest productions, I must particularly request my readers not to be too censorious in judging them, as some were written when I was a mere boy.

"A Dream of Christmas" and other minor Poems appeared in *Once a Month* and in the columns of the local press.

I received the thanks of H.R.H, the Prince of Wales for the Poem on the marriage of His Royal Highness with Princess Alexandra, and who was graciously pleased to accept the said Poem.

JOSEPH PULLEN COLLINS.

Chesnut Tree House,
Leytonstone,
March, 1871.

CONTENTS.

War 1

On the Marriage of the Princess Louise with the
    Marquis of Lorne, a Bridal Ode............... 7

A Summer's Day.. 11

A Cry from Lancashire 12

Alexandra, Our Danish Flower, a National Song 16

The Bee 19

Welcome to Alexandra 20

On the Marriage of the Prince of Wales with
    Princess Alexandra, a Nuptial Ode 22

What do the People Want with Reform, a Non-
    Reformer's Song 25

On the Chignon 31

The Queen of the May, a May-Day Song........ 33

Would I were a Fairy Queen....................... 36

A Dream of Christmas............................... 38

The Daisy... 43

The Honeysuckle 44

Havelock the Brave 45

Ode to the Bard of Avon............................ 47

W A R !

" Cry havoc, let's slip the dogs of war."—*Shakespeare.*

Hark ! hark ! it is the war-cry

That across the sea we hear,

Which brings tears to a mother's eye

And fills each heart with fear.

When we think of those we love to greet,

Who are marching on to war,

Fearless of their fate the foe they meet,

We might never see them more

Or hear that familiar voice again,

For they may ne'er return to the happy home,

But die upon the battle plain

Leaving fatherless ones at home.

On the bloody field those dear ones lay

Among the dying and the dead,

Trampled on by flying foemen deeper in the clay

And then left on the field for dead.

There in the green valley the warrior lies

Who has fought and died for his country's sake :

He breathes a dear name before he dies.

Who will to his dear friends the sad news break,

No one was near to hear his cries

For help.   Will no one come ?

His prayer was heard, of his wound he dies.

The angels now will come

To bear him to their Lord above

In that happy land of rest

Where He will bless him with his love,

And his soul at peace will rest.

A fair-haired girl in mourning clad

Was kneeling by a new made grave,

The tears fell from those eyes so sad

Uponher father's grave,

And in her grief for him she loved most dear,

She threw herself upon the grave

Where fell the orphan's tear.

She strewsthe grave with lillies white

And plants flower-wreaths, as well,

Glory sheds its hallowed light

Where her dead father fell.

Those golden ears of corn are trodden by the foe

And the green valleys are dyed with life's crimson

     gore,

The enemy are charging as they go,

As they are marching on to war.

Those peaceful homesteads where rural bliss abound

And woodbines entwine about its cosy portch,

Is now in ashes on the ground

Destroyed by the incendiary's torch,

And the inmates, too, were put to death

By the enemy's ruthless hand.

How bravely they met their death

In their fatherland.

Thou fated city thou art destined to fall,

But defend its ramparts to the last.

Let every man answer bravely to the call

When they hear the trumpet's blast.

Will none to Paris some assistance lend

And drive the invaders from her shore.

Alas, no assistance will they send

To help her in this bloody war.

Misery and starvationstares them in the face,

No bread,no bread, is still the cry.

Oh, Father in Heaven given them grace

To conquer, or of starvation they will die.

Hundreds are dying within those fated walls

Of hunger in the bitter cold.

Shot and shell assail the walls

Of the fine and noble city

Now wrecked in its grandeur and life

But they cannot be bereft of all pity

For the poor unfortunate wife.

Flow on: flow on, beautiful Rhine,

May peace soon reign along its shores,

Thou land of the vine with its luscious entwine

About its vineyards near its shores,

Strew lillies o'er the warrior's grave

And let him rest in peace,

Weave laurels for the brave,

And let this bloody conflict cease.

Oh God, we pray thee, end this dreadful strife,

Throw down the sword and peace proclaim once
    more,

Look with pity on the widowed wife

And draw the curtain upon those agonising scenes
    of war.

ON THE '

ARRIAGE OF THE PRINCESS LOUISE

WITH THE

MARQUIS OF LORNE.

A BRIDAL ODE.

Hail, hail, hail, thou son of Campbell's clan,

From bonnie Scotland far has come

To wed the daughter of our Queen :

The Son of Argyle is the chosen one,

To be her partner in love's fond dream,

He takes her blushing to his heart

His fair and beauteous wife,

Those loving hearts death alone shall part,

In their fond dream of life.

Heaven bless the youthful pair,

Who on the wedding day,

Will join both heart and hand,

At God's altar on that day

As man and wife shall stand.

Orange blossoms and lilies white

Shall grace that snow white brow,

Far purer than the gems so bright,

That adorns our Princess now.

Hark, the wedding bells are merrily ringing,

And waft their charm upon the morning breeze,

See the Spring flowers that the bride's-maids are
    bringing

To adorn our Princess—the fair Louise.

Bless her ! the fair young bride,

And kiss away that falling tear

That the heart would scorn to hide,

When she leaves that mother dear

A young and blushing bride.

May the future now hidden and dark,

Unfold one fond dream of love,

Never to be destroyed by Time's hoary mark,

That one pure dream of love.

Spring bursts forth in all its gorgeous array,

Flowers with their perfume rent the air,

On that happy wedding day.

When the son of Argyle shall our Princess bear

To the Highlands far away.

A SUMMER'S DAY.

———o———

I LOVE to roam through the sweet green fields

    And see the lambs so blithe and gay

That skip about the sweet green fields

    Early on a summer's day

I love to hear the birds singing in the trees,

    The murmuring of the waters and the whispering
        of the leaves,

The chanting of the skylark and the humming of the
        bees,

    Among the summer flowers and the sweet green
        leaves

A CRY FROM LANCASHIRE.

———o———

Hark ! it is the cry from Lancashire,

　　Mingled with sorrow and with pain,

The wretched mother with her infant share,

　　Proffered shelter from the rain.

A mother's love to soothe its care

　　Through the busy scenes of life

And worldly strife, and share

　　Its mother's wretched life.

Hark ! it is the cry from Lancashire

　　Of the homeless, and at home,

Who are starving, while we share

    The comforts of a home.

To preserve her offspring's tender life

    The mother begs from door to door

To get the bread of life

    For the sleeping babe she bore.

Whose wasted form clasps the infant to her breast

    To give it sustenance its life to sustain,

She laid its sleeping form to rest

    Whilst hunger did her body pain.

She had been out some food to seek,

    But had not been successful on the way,

For, lo, her constitution was, from exhaustion, weak

    She had had nothing all that day.

The wretched mother would fall on her knees and
    pray

    To her God to give her bread.

As her poor babe in her arms did lay

    Cold as if t'was dead.

On them had been laid the cold hand of death,

    She shivered under that chilly hand.

The little babe gave up its fleeting breath

    To Heaven to meet the angelic band.

" My child, my child," the weeping mother cried,

    " It is thy mother who to thee speaks."

She did not know the child had died,

    The little lamb above the angels seeks.

No, not dead, my own dear child,

The tears ran down her pale cheek.

She kissed the clay-cold body of her child

And cried, we shall again in heaven meet.

The mother had just breathed her last,

The night bird screeched

And all the busy life had from her past,

Her soul had the eternal heavens reached.

There laid both mother and child alone,

Rocked fast in death's embrace

While the moon through the window shone

A lustre on death's pale face.

ALEXANDRA OUR DANISH FLOWER.

———o———

A National Song.

Along our British shore

　　Let ten thousand voices shower

A welcome from old England

　　To Alexandra our Danish flower.

Long may she in happiness be

　　And peaceful days in store,

Or ne'er an hour of trouble see,

　　Our future Queen adore.

Along our British shore

　　Let ten thousand voices shower

A welcome from old England

    To Alexandra our Danish flower

If danger should us threaten

    At any distant day,

Let them who dare attack us

    Britannia will keep at bay.

Long may they live in peaceful times

    Ne'er know any but the happy day,

When a wreath of orange blossoms entwines

    On the brow of the fair Alexandra.

Along our British shore

    Let ten thousand voices shower

A welcome from old England,

    To Alexandra our Danish flower.

God bless that Danish flower

That is planted in our isle,

May her beauty never wither

Nor from her face that smile,

But may her health and love combine

Until that happy day

When a crown of gold shall shine

On the brow of Queen Alexandra.

Along our British shore

Let ten thousand voices shower

A blessing from old England,

On Alexandra our Danish flower.

THE BEE.

———o———

Oh, gentle, little busy bee

On a summer's day may see

Gathering honey from flower to flower,

And buzzing round the clematis bower.

Ah ! a pattern to the sluggard be,

Ever industrious, ever free,

In and out the busy hive

With loaded treasures they arrive.

WELCOME TO ALEXANDRA.

On her Entry into London.

————o————

Welcome the Danish flower,

   To London now has come,

With all her loveliness and gentle power,

   To wed Victoria's son.

Let cheering greet her on the way,

   As she in her carriage pass

With smiles she holds the sway

   Along the peopled mass.

The cannons roar and the bells do ring,

    Banners flying and decorations grand,

May this happy union bring

    Her joy and happiness in our land.

ON THE

MARRIAGE OF THE PRINCE OF WALES

WITH

PRINCESS ALEXANDRA.

A NUPTIAL ODE.

HARK! the distant trumpets sound,

Gorgeous ceremonial abound;

It is the nuptials of our Prince of Wales,

Let its welcome echo through the distant vales;

And with it honour and loyalty share,

Banners fluttering through the air.

Princes, dukes, assembled there,

Organ sends forth its music rare,

Thro' the chapel's sepulchre air.

The Bridegroom alights near the chapel door,

Chanting by St. George's choir.

How well he looks ! and his stately bearing

In Colonel's uniform and order wearing :

A plumed hat he carries in his hand

Amidst the music and scene so grand.

Albert Edward waits the coming of his Bride,

Leaning patiently at the altar side.

Alexandra, thy bride, is coming down the aisle ;

She looks pale, but yet a faint smile

Was vivid on her pretty face.

No fairer form could nature trace,

Robed in tulle and silk so white,

With orange blossoms and rosebuds light ;

And on her pretty hair was sparkling bright

A diamond tiara of gems so rare

Reclining on a brow so fair.

Followed by her bridal maids, who bore

The wedding bouquet, the marriage to adore

Happy, happy, happy pair !

None but he deserves her care.

The cry re-echoes from the distant vales—

God bless the Prince and Princess of Wales !

WHAT DO THE PEOPLE WANT WITH REFORM?

———o———

A Non-Reformer's Song.

" What do the people want with Reform ?" is the cry

Through every city around.

Can you tell the reason why

Such discontent abound

n the hearts of working men.

It is not a vote you want, but let them relieve

Thy starving family, they'll not look on them,

But they thy position only will deceive

By telling you it's Reform you want,

    And lead you on to destruction to the end

With misery staring you in the face, they'll not supply
    thy daily want.

But to a prison they will send.

    What do the people want is the question.

    Reform, Reform—cease that cry.

    And why such meetings of indignation,

    Can they tell the reason why.

Disperse thy followers and bring thy standard down,

    Why should we thus meet

In every city and in every town,

    Parading idly through each street,

Dressed in gaudy sashes and banners bear.

Be satisfied and leave well alone.

Thou misguided men do have a care,

Think upon the little ones at home.

Let thy motto be, Work, Work, and be Content

With thy position on life's road,

Do not be discontented with what is meant

To bring happiness to thy next abode.

What do the people want is the question,

Reform, Reform—cease that cry,

And why such meetings of indignation,

Can they tell the reason why.

Working men of England, supporters of the State,

If you toil your efforts will be crowned,

And do not thy exertions abate

Until thy coffers shall abound

With wealth, and then you'll a position gain.

It is then time enough to talk about the rulers of our
land.

You would then look on with disgust what you are
now seeking to obtain.

Then have the same opinion now, and dont let other
views stand

In the way of progress, but onward go,

And show that the British workman have the good
sense to know

The friends to his country, and have no wish to make a
foe

Of those who, for thy country's good, great mea-
sures do bestow.

What do the people want is the question,

Reform, Reform—cease that cry,

Let peace reign, instead of indignation,

And progress and plenty be the cry.

May peace reign through our little isle,

And our barns with corn be stored,

May fortune on the deserving smile

And scatter Reform abroad,

But if war should rage in this happy land.

The British workman would be the foremost in the band

To defend his country he bleeds and falls,

And on the battle-field would die.

But if he recovers he is ready when duty calls,

And into danger is the foremost one to fly.

While loving hearts are with excitement beating,

    Then plant the laurel wreath upon his brow, and
      let it rest.

He lives, his wife and little ones are greeting

    Him with his medals on his breast.

    May peace reign through our little isle,

    And our barns with corn be stored,

    May fortune on the deserving smile,

    And scatter Reform abroad.

ON THE CHIGNON.

————o————

WHAT is that on the ladies' heads I see,

That surely cannot the fashion be.

But they are never going to be so absurd

To wear that, no, really that is too absurd.

Why thus outrage nature and wear another head.

Leave it off, and let your golden tresses hang instead

Down your neck so fair,

Or with ribbons blue tie up your hair.

Oh, ladies fair, why do you wear

That mass of artificial hair.

Which underneath your bonnet shows.

Its utility I am sure no one knows.

" It's the fashion," the ladies cry,

To leave it off, we cannot, and why?

Because it's so hideous and do not become

Your beauty, my fair but knowing one.

THE QUEEN OF THE MAY..

———o———

A May Day Song.

On one May morning there was seen

   A maiden brisk and smart,

Was hurrying away to the maypole green

   Quite cheerful and light at heart,

To join in the dance around the May.

   She wore a robe of muslin light

Trimmed with ribbons blue

   And rosebuds red and white,

And lilies and May blossoms, too,

   Was to adorn our Queen of the May.

Chorus.—Around the May they merrily go,

An homage to the Queen they pay,

Around the May they merrily go,

Early on a bright May day.

A lily entwined her flaxen hair,

Which was beautiful in curl,

The villagers as they pass did stare,

At this pretty blue-eyed girl,

She was the Queen of the May,

Her lips were like the ruby,

A kiss they would entice,

For a loving heart had she,

And she was chosen twice

Their Queen of the May.

Chorus.—Around the May they merrily go,

An homage to the Queen they pay,

Around the May they merrily go,

Early on a bright May day.

WOULD I WERE A FAIRY QUEEN.

———o———

Would I were a Fairy Queen

And roam where lillies grow,

In mossy caverns I love to dwell,

Where the crystal waters flow

At the bottom of the dell.

I'll throw aside all dull care,

And live in that happy land,

What happiness can you compare

With that of the fairy band.

They'll with flowers deck me,

With ribbons of colours bright,

A star of gems so rare,

And lilies of spotless white

Will adorn my flaxen hair.

Then I'll throw aside all dull care,

And live in that happy land,

What happiness can you compare

With that of the fairy band.

A DREAM OF CHRISTMAS.

———ô———

THE holly cart parades the street

With mistletoe, laurel and bay,

Laid together in a tangled heap

For the adornment of Christmas Day.

The red-breasted robin has no place to go,

With ruffled feathers he hops in the snow,

The leafless trees and bushes, too;

The red berried holly a cheerfulness threw

On the frozen ground

Of the dreary landscape round.

What shelter have the little birds got,

No greenwood bower or shady grot,

No running streams or secluded nooks,

Nothing but leafless trees and frozen brooks.

The snow was falling thickly on the ground,

The bleak wind blew a hurricane round

The corners of a street

Where little ones with shoeless feet

Were shivering with the cold,

And what a sad story the eye and cheek betold :

No home had they to seek for rest,

No mother dear to soothe the aching breast,

Darkness was throwing its dark mantle o'er the earth,

Things looked grand and all was mirth,

But the poor little wanderers no comfort had they

To look forward to the coming of Christmas Day.

Hark ! that the waits must be

Near the little holly tree.

Christmas is now coming in,

The wassail bowl along do bring,

Fill'd with nice spiced wine up to the brim,

And on the surface lemon in slices swim,

Drink ye all, and merry, too,

Welcome Christmas, all of ye,

Who comes amongst us once in every year,

And brings with him such lots of cheer.

Come lads, bring the yule log in,

For the festive preparations let all begin.

Trumpets sound and the kettle-drums roll,

Announces the approach of the Lord of Misrule,

Who, with wand in hand, he leads the way

Of the mummers of the day.

The carols are sung at the manor-house door

In commemoration of the day we all adore.

Come, bring the red holly, laurel and bay,

From the hall where clusters lay,

For the oak partition to decorate,

This festive season to celebrate.

A bough of mistletoe hangs in the hall,

The red-berried holly covers the oak-pannelled wall

Where under the mistletoe the lasses are led

By the lads, who must have a kiss, but instead

They shake and toss their curls with sad disdain,

That Giles and George are afraid to try again.

The ringers assemble at the ivy-covered tower

Of the village-church at the midnight hour

To chime those merry Christmas bells,

How many a true tale their music tells.

Larders are stocked with Christmas fare,

Turkeys, geese. ducks, and poultry rare,

Barons of beef, and the head of a boar,

For the Christmas banquet to adore,

The brawny pudding, with its condiment so nice,

And pies of mince and puddings of rice,

The manor-house, what luxuries on its table laid !

What preparations there are made.

For this festive season alone ;

In the humble cottage there is sometimes none.

But, however poor, you will sure to see

A little sprig of nature's Christmas tree.

THE DAISY.

———o———

Peeping above the grassy plat

A white bell with a purple cap,

With a green slender stalk,

Bordering along the gravel walk.

Growing in clusters there are seen

On the soft velvet green,

Closing its pretty head at night,

And opening again at morning light.

THE HONEYSUCKLE.

———— o ————

The honeysuckle, the charming flower,

Inclining round the little ivy bower,

With its perfume rents the air

Through the garden everywhere.

Hanging in clusters from the top

Where the buds and flowers drop

Near the little rustic seat,

Where the lovers often meet.

HAVELOCK THE BRAVE.

———— o ————

H-ENRY HAVELOCK, the bravest of the brave,

A-t Lucknow did the sufferers save,

V-aliant and courageous were his men.

E-very man and woman blessed him when

L-ucknow was relieved from misery and pain.

O-n his brow the laurel-wreath of victory plant.

C-ountless honours he ought to obtain,

K-ingly riches and titles triumphant.

T-he hero has the sword resigned,

H-e will a peaceful heaven find,

E-verlasting peace and glory there combined.

B-earing the hero the angels take their flight,

R-obed in vestures of spotless white,

A-nd to that happy land the hero 's led,

V-ictory crown that plant upon his head

E-verlasting light of glory shall around him shed.

ODE TO THE BARD OF AVON.

In Commemoration of his Tercentenary.

————o————

It's now three hundred years and more

Since the birth of him we all adore,

Who, under a monument of marble lies

Pointing upward to the skies;

Whose hallowed bones are turned to dust,

Are mingled with the earth, and must

Be mouldered quite away.

Where the yew trees growing high,

The gentle Avon flowing by,

Where an awful stillness reigns

Along the grassy mounds and plains.

O ! thou Poet of love divine,

What shall we offer to thy shrine ?

A monument of literary fame

Has already been raised to thy name.

Whose works are read and sought

From the cottage to the court,

The Muses, his sacred relics, save.

Stands guarding by the Poet's grave.